A JOSH McINTIRE BOOK

UNDERGROUND HERO

Elaine K. McEwan

Chariot Books™
David C. Cook Publishing Co.

9734

Chariot Books™ is an imprint of David C. Cook Publishing Co.
David C. Cook Publishing Co., Elgin, Illinois 60120
David C. Cook Publishing Co., Weston, Ontario
Nova Distribution, Ltd., Torquay, England

UNDERGROUND HERO
© 1993 by Elaine K. McEwan

Cover design by Elizabeth Thompson
Cover illustration by Robert Papp
First printing, 1993
Printed in the United States of America
97 96 95 94 93   5 4 3 2 1

Library of Congress Cataloging-in-Publication Data
McEwan, Elaine K.
    Underground Hero: a Josh McIntire Book/ by Elaine K.
McEwan
    p. cm.   "A Josh McIntire book"--P.
    Summary: Ten-year-old Josh learns the value of prayer when
dealing with his parents' divorce and when he gets in trouble
for investigating a house that may have been a stop on the
Underground Railroad.
    ISBN 0-7814-0113-5
    [1. Divorce--Fiction. 2. Christian life--Fiction.]   I. Title.
PZ7.M4784545Un   1993
[Fic]--dc20   92-27104
                                                   CIP
                                                   AC

The Klum house was just across the field. From a distance it looked pretty impressive, but once we got closer, I could see the peeling paint and boarded-up windows. I got a little chill.

"Who lived there?" I asked Ben.

"My dad said that old man Klum died five years ago and hadn't paid his taxes. Now the house belongs to the county. They want to turn it into a museum or something."

We stood in what was once the front yard, overgrown with dried weeds and shrubs. The porch steps were crumbling. Just then the sun vanished behind a cloud. I shivered again.

"So what are we going to do?" Ben asked.

"Just walk around and look at it, I guess," I said.

"Aw, we've got to see the inside," said Ben. "How will we know if this really was an Underground Railroad stop if we don't go inside?"

I hesitated a moment. I really should have called my mom before I left.

"C'mon, Josh," Ben prodded. "Don't be a wimp. . . ."

Ask for these titles from Chariot Family Publishing:
Project Cockroach
The Best Defense
Adam Straight to the Rescue
Adam Straight and the Mysterious Neighbor
Mystery on Mirror Mountain
Courage on Mirror Mountain
Mystery at Deepwood Bay

To Emily

Underground Hero was inspired by
The Underground Railroad in DuPage County, Illinois
by Glennette Tilley Turner, © 1980
Newman Educational Publishers, Wheaton, IL

The phone was ringing when I unlocked the front door. I dropped my book bag and raced to answer it.

Back in my old home in Woodview, I never got butterflies in my stomach when the phone rang. I just picked it up and said, "Hello, this is the McIntire residence." But since my parents got divorced and my mom and I moved to Grandville, a ringing phone always gives me a funny feeling in my stomach. I keep wanting it to be my dad and it hardly ever is.

"Hello, this is the McIntire residence."

"Hi, Joshua."

"Oh, hi, Mom." I hoped she couldn't hear the disappointment in my voice.

"Just checking in. Have any homework?"

"Nothing much," I replied. "Just a little social studies report on the Underground Railroad."

"Well, you can tell me all about it when I get home," she said hurriedly. "I have another call."

Mom works at Associated Foods and has to

answer the phone for her boss.

When I went back to get my book bag, I saw the package on the front porch. It was wrapped in brown paper and addressed to me. There was no return address, but I recognized the handwriting—my dad's. My stomach did a flip flop. I picked up the package and shook it. It felt empty. Should I wait until Mom came home to open it? Nah, it was addressed to me.

I'd been concentrating so hard on the package that I didn't hear someone come up the porch steps.

"What's the matter?" asked Wendell. "You look weird."

Wendell had his nerve calling me weird. He's my next door neighbor, and he takes the gold medal for weirdness. Or at least he used to, until I convinced him to start wearing T-shirts once in awhile instead of his button-down plaids. Now he almost looks normal.

"I got a package from my dad," I said.

"Great! Open it," Wendell replied.

I felt apprehensive. That was a new word I'd learned in fifth grade. If you're apprehensive about something, you're kind of scared about it. Part of me wanted to open the package right away and part of me was worried about what might be inside. I guess I was afraid of being disappointed. I wasn't sure that I wanted to open it in front of Wendell, either.

8

"I think I'll wait until my mom comes home," I said.

Wendell seemed to accept that idea and changed the subject.

"So, whaddya think of the social studies assignment?"

Most kids talk about TV shows and sports teams, but Wendell always talks about school. I guess that's one of the other weird things about him. He actually enjoys doing homework.

"I'd never heard of the Underground Railroad until Mrs. Bannister talked about it today," I said. "I don't get it."

Wendell sort of scrunched up his face and began explaining. I could tell this lecture was going to be longer than Mrs. Bannister's had been. Wendell doesn't always know when to quit. I think he'll be a professor when he grows up.

"Wen, if you don't mind, could we wait until later? I've got to do my homework before Awana," I pleaded.

He looked disappointed. I felt a little guilty about hurting his feelings, but I needed some time alone to open that package before Mom got home.

"See you later," he said. "I'll come by for you at 7:15."

We had Awana every Tuesday night at Wendell's church. It was really my church too, I guess. I'd

9

started going every week after I'd asked Jesus into my life. Now that I was a Christian, I was supposed to go to church regularly. At least that's what Wendell said. This Christian stuff wasn't as easy as he made it look, but he was pretty good about not lecturing me.

With Wendell gone, the queasy feeling in my stomach came back. It was now or never. I tried to rip through the heavy strapping tape that secured the paper. My dad had done a good wrapping job. I was going to need a crowbar to open this one.

My heart was pounding. Would there be a letter inside? It wasn't my birthday for another three months. The box didn't offer much of a clue, unless my dad was sending me oil filters. He must be selling auto parts again.

I dumped the contents out on the floor and tore through the tissue paper. There were some pieces of wood in a plastic bag and an envelope. I couldn't figure it out. I picked up the plastic bag and read the paper insert. It was a balsa wood airplane model. Now I was excited. I'd never had one before. I ripped open the envelope.

I couldn't believe it. It was actually a letter from my dad.

Dear Joshua,

You're probably wondering what's been happening to your old dad, but I've had a pretty rough couple of months.

I was glad that he'd had a rough time, because it

hadn't exactly been a picnic for me either. I kept wondering what was wrong with me and thinking he didn't like me anymore. He'd only called twice since we moved here.

You probably think you're to blame for what's happened, but your old dad is pretty much of a jerk.

Now I was confused. I wasn't used to hearing my dad talk like that. Dads were supposed to be strong and know everything. What did he mean?

I'm sending a little present to remind you of me. I used to love model airplanes when I was your age.

Then why didn't he give me one a long time ago? My mind was racing. This letter wasn't making me feel as good as I thought it would. I'd rather have my mom and dad together than some crummy model airplane. I could feel myself getting mad, and the tears began to well up in my eyes. I almost wanted to take the package and break it in two over my knee.

Then I remembered what my friend Sonny Studebaker told me. I work for Sonny in his leather shop. Sonny says that when you feel like crying and know you should be brave, prayer and karate are the two best things to do.

Well, I could give the model airplane a karate chop and finish it off for good, and then I could pray for my mom and dad to get back together again. But somehow I didn't think that Master Lee, my karate teacher, would think much of my busting up a little

11

balsa wood airplane. He'd probably suggest saving my strength for the yellow belt test that was coming up.

And my prayers so far to get Mom and Dad back together hadn't worked. Wendell said that God hears all of our prayers, but He sure wasn't getting back to me very fast on this one. But I whispered one more prayer, just to show Him I wasn't holding a grudge.

Dear God, I just want to go back to Woodview and be a family again. Could you please do it by Christmas? It's November now and that gives You a whole month. I'm sorry I got mad. Thanks, God.

I felt more calm. Maybe Sonny was right about prayer. Now I had to decide whether to show the letter to Mom. She'd been smiling a little more lately, and it didn't seem fair to spoil that. I gathered up the mess and stuffed it in the back of my closet. Then I tucked the letter in my jeans and went to the kitchen for a snack.

My mind went back to the social studies assignment. Maybe I was turning weird like Wendell, thinking about schoolwork. But Mrs. Bannister had a way of making even the dullest subjects interesting. We were going to visit a museum and have an author come to our class. She'd written a book about the Underground Railroad in Illinois. At least that was something to look forward to. And maybe I'd try putting the model airplane together.

The grandfather clock in the hall chimed four. I knew I'd better get that snack before Mom came home, or she'd say I was spoiling my dinner. I needed to review my Awana stuff, too. There were a lot of Bible verses and stuff to memorize if I wanted to get my badges.

There wasn't much left in the refrigerator. Back in Woodview we'd always had lots of good junk to eat. Mom even made cookies once a week. She says we're trying to be healthier now, but I know it's because we don't have much extra money. I spread some peanut butter and jelly on a piece of toast, stuffed the whole thing in my mouth, and settled down at the kitchen table with my Awana book. I liked eating alone sometimes. You didn't have to worry about table manners. A big glob of grape jelly came squirting out of my mouth and landed on the table. It just stood there quivering in the sunlight.

I noticed the bright blue of the sky and how the oak tree was losing its leaves, and all of a sudden I felt good again. It was the strangest thing. How could I go from being ready to cry to feeling good in just five minutes?

Samantha Sullivan didn't start out to be one of my friends. In fact when I first got to know her, I couldn't stand her. She was the bossiest person I'd ever met. But she was in my cooperative group, and Mrs. Bannister forced us to work together until we got along. Now I don't mind her at all and besides, her mother makes the best chocolate brownies I've ever eaten. Whenever Samantha brings them in her lunch, she sneaks one to me when nobody's looking.

Today we were getting into new groups, and I hoped it wouldn't be as traumatic this time. Traumatic is another new word I've learned this year. My mom says it's traumatic for kids when their parents get divorced. I guess when something is really upsetting, it's traumatic. Once Samantha and I got into a big fight, and I ended up running away from school. That was definitely traumatic. But I've changed a lot since then. Anyway, I hope so.

The bell had rung, but Mrs. Bannister wasn't in the classroom. This was highly unusual, as Mrs.

Bannister is a person who hates to waste time. She's always talking about the importance of time-on-task. I think it's an idea she got at some meeting.

"Where do you suppose Mrs. Bannister is?" Samantha asked.

"Maybe she's sick and we have a substitute," said Maria.

Just then Mrs. Bannister sailed through the doorway with her springy gray curls bouncing away and her glasses and fountain pens jingling around her neck. But she was not alone. From all appearances, I would no longer be the new kid in the room.

The new boy looked different. Not weird like Wendell, just different. At first I wasn't sure why. He was smiling and looked friendly, and he had a great Chicago Bears T-shirt on. I wondered if he liked the quarterback Brent Hillman.

Then I figured it out. We'd had a special class at my old school, where all of the kids were different. I wondered why this boy wasn't in a special class here in Grandville with other kids just like him.

"Class, I'd like you to meet Trevor Monroe," said Mrs. Bannister. "He just moved to Grandville from Woodview. You came from Woodview, didn't you, Joshua? Did you know Trevor?"

Mrs. Bannister looked in my direction, and I shook my head. I hoped the rest of the class wouldn't think that I hung out with kids like Trevor. It was hard

15

enough being friends with Wendell.

"Trevor and his mom are going to take a tour of the school, and then he'll be back to join us."

A pretty, dark-haired lady came in and left with Trevor.

Mrs. Bannister had a serious look on her face as she stood at the front of the room. "Class, we're going to have a wonderful opportunity in 5B this year."

Oh no, I thought. Whenever my mom talked about wonderful opportunities, it meant we were going to do something that she thought was great and I thought was dumb.

"Welcoming Trevor into our class is the wonderful opportunity," she continued. "You'll probably notice right away that Trevor has a hard time doing some of the things we do and that he looks a little different from us. That's because he has Down's syndrome. But I expect each of you to treat Trevor just exactly the same way you treat one another in this class—with respect."

Maybe Mrs. Bannister was hallucinating. We weren't always that nice to each other. It had been pretty tough when I was new. I had to prove myself playing dodge ball. I hoped Trevor knew what he was up against.

"Before we have science today," Mrs. Bannister went on, "we're going to form new cooperative groups. I've been so pleased with the way some of you have learned to work together." She smiled in the direction of our group.

I found myself thinking that I might even miss Samantha and her bossy ways.

"As I read off the names of the new groups, start moving your desks around," directed Mrs. Bannister. "Joshua McIntire, Tracy Kendall . . ."

My brain stopped functioning when I heard Tracy's name read after mine. This was my lucky day. Tracy was one of the neatest girls in the class. She went to Wendell's church. I sat staring into space, unable to move.

Mrs. Bannister was talking to me. "Joshua, are you awake?"

"I'm sorry, Mrs. Bannister, I didn't hear you," I stammered.

"I said, start moving your desk over there," she said firmly. She pointed to the far side of the room where Tracy and Sarah Perez were already sitting.

I could feel my face getting red. "Sure, Mrs. Bannister, right away."

I wondered who the other boy in my new group would be. I hoped it wasn't someone that Tracy would like better than me. I slid my desk across from hers.

"Hi, Josh," Tracy said quietly.

"Hi, Tracy," I answered. While I was busy trying to impress her, I didn't notice who was moving his desk next to me. It was Trevor. He must have come back from his tour of the school already.

Oh, no, I thought. *Now I'm going to have to baby-sit.*

"Hi, Trevor," Tracy said quietly. She gave him a big smile and stuck out her hand. She hadn't shook hands with me. Not to be outdone, I shook hands with Trevor too. He gave me a wide smile. He sure was a happy person.

"Class, may I have your attention, please?" said Mrs. Bannister. "We've taken enough time getting into groups. We need to start science. We're doing owl pellets today."

I'd heard a sixth grader talking about this project. It really sounded sickening. I wondered how Tracy and Sarah were going to handle it. Fortunately they had me, Joshua the Brave, to help them. I could impress Tracy right away.

Mrs. Bannister was passing out some work sheets, and Ben Anderson walked behind her handing out disgusting brown things that looked like big walnuts. They'd been soaking in a pail of water at the back of the room.

I couldn't believe Mrs. Bannister was asking Ben to help her. He'd probably put a wet pellet down Samantha's back when she wasn't looking.

Looking at the gushy mess in front of me, I no longer felt like Joshua the Brave.

"Isn't this great?" said Tracy to Trevor. "We're going to take this apart and find bones inside of it."

Sarah looked like she was going to be sick, and I

didn't feel that terrific myself. Trevor was still smiling at Tracy.

"Joshua's going to help you," Tracy said to Trevor.

"Yeah, sure," I replied grudgingly. I couldn't let Tracy see how I really felt.

Mrs. Bannister was at the front of the room talking. I had to listen if I was going to do Trevor's work too.

"This pellet contains undigested portions of food items consumed by owls and regurgitated as a compact mass through their mouths," explained Mrs. Bannister.

"That means the owl vomited," Tracy explained to our group in a loud whisper. She looked like she was actually enjoying this lesson.

Mrs. Bannister went on. "The pellet you have contains the materials the owl couldn't digest, like bones, beaks, claws, or teeth of mammals, birds, reptiles, amphibians, and fish; the head parts, thorax, or wing cases of insects; seed husks and other coarse vegetable materials."

A loud voice came from across the room. I recognized it as Ben's.

"You mean an owl barfed up all that in one little ball?"

"I beg your pardon, Ben," said Mrs. Bannister, with a frown. "You won't find every single thing I mentioned, but many of them. Those things will be on the inside. The softer items such as fur, bird feathers, and vegetable fibers are on the outside."

I was glad that lunch was still a couple of hours away, as my stomach was absolutely churning. Tracy, on the other hand, looked like she was in heaven. All I could think of was some poor little mouse getting swallowed whole by a big nasty barn owl, and Tracy was ready to win the Nobel Prize in science.

"What do we do with the bones once we take the pellet apart?" asked Tracy excitedly.

I wondered if I could get a case of the chicken pox or measles and get sent home by the nurse. I was probably going to throw up anyhow. I hoped the class would think it was the flu.

Trevor touched my arm. "I don't understand," he said quietly. "What do I do?" He looked kind of desperate, and for a minute I forgot about how I felt.

"Don't worry," I said. "I'll help you."

Trevor gave me another big grin. He made me feel really important.

Mrs. Bannister responded to Tracy's question. "I'm glad you're thinking ahead, Tracy. Each group is going to keep track of the kinds of bones they find in their pellets, and then we'll all draw some conclusions about what kinds of animals barn owls eat most often."

My mind was wandering again. All I could think of was everyone in class throwing up their cafeteria lunch and counting the number of corn kernels we found. If I didn't stop thinking, I really would be sick.

"Then," Mrs. Bannister went on, "we're going to assemble the bones into a skeleton and paste them with our Elmer's on these sheets of black paper. They'll make a wonderful display for open house."

"Yuck!" Samantha screeched. "Who'll want to see some dry old bones at open house?"

No one but Tracy seemed to think this was a great assignment.

"I'm going to pass out the teasing needles now," said Mrs. Bannister.

That got a laugh from the class, but Mrs. Bannister jumped right in. "That doesn't mean you're going to tease each other with these," she said. "They are just wire probes to help you take apart the pellets. You can also use your fingers."

I could hear one of the girls giggling as Ben poked her with a teasing needle. After a stern look from Mrs. Bannister, he stopped. His behavior had improved a lot in the last month.

"Let's get started," suggested Mrs. Bannister. "We have lots to do before lunch."

At the mention of food, my stomach did another loop-the-loop. Throwing up was not going to impress Tracy Kendall.

"Are you okay, Joshua?" she asked. "You're not sick, are you?"

I wished she would just ignore me.

Just then Trevor picked up his teasing needle and

held it above the pellet. "What do I do?" he asked again.

I didn't know whether he was kidding or serious. But then it dawned on me. Trevor really didn't know. He'd had a hard time understanding everything the teacher had just said. He really was going to need my help.

"Just do what I do," I said.

I picked up my teasing needle and began to cautiously poke at the disgusting pellet. I couldn't be sick and help Trevor at the same time.

"Try to find the skulls first," instructed Mrs. Bannister. "Then you'll know what kind of mammal your owl ate."

Once Trevor got the idea that he was supposed to open up the pellet there was no stopping him.

"Look what I found!" he shouted. He held up a tiny skull, and I gave him a big smile.

The morning flew by as Trevor and I poked around in our owl pellets and assembled our skeletons. I had a vole skeleton and Trevor had a mole. I began to forget that Trevor was different. It made me feel really good to help him.

I was only worried about one thing. Tracy Kendall probably thought I was a wimp.

I turned out the light and lay in the darkness trying to pray. It's hard when I'm tired—I get started and then my mind starts to wander. I thought about all the stuff that had happened in one week. The letter from Dad, Trevor and Tracy in my cooperative group, my yellow belt test coming up, and the Underground Railroad.

Tomorrow was Saturday, and Mom had to work overtime. Sonny's shop would be closed because he had a concert out of town. He's a drummer in a Christian rock band. Wendell and his folks were driving to Michigan to visit his grandma. Looked like I'd be on my own.

Another kid I know went to visit his dad on weekends. I wished I could do that. I decided I'd give Ben Anderson a call. We could work on our social studies project together. Neither Wendell nor my mom would give that idea a thumbs-up, given Ben's history of being not-such-a-good influence on me, but they didn't have to spend a whole Saturday by themselves. I felt deserted.

Next thing I knew Mom was shaking my shoulder.

"Josh, I'm leaving for the office in fifteen minutes. I left some fruit and cereal on the counter for you. I'm sorry I have to work today."

"That's okay, Mom," I answered. "I have a lot to do today."

"Like what?" she asked. "I don't want you getting into any trouble."

"Aw, Mom, you don't have to worry."

"I wish that were the case, Josh," she answered with a frown. "But you've had more than your share of problems since we moved here."

"I'll be fine," I assured her.

She brushed a kiss against the top of my head and squeezed my shoulder.

"I love you, Josh," she said. "I don't know what I'd do if anything happened to you."

I was glad that she was on her way out the door. I didn't want her to see the tears in my eyes. Suddenly it struck me that Thanksgiving was only a couple weeks away—our first Thanksgiving without Dad. I wondered where we'd spend the day. And who would carve the turkey?

The long day stretched in front of me. I decided

to eat breakfast, wash the dishes, and make my bed. That would impress Mom. When I finished, I dumped out my book bag and tried to find the Underground Railroad assignment sheet. Instead I found a math paper I'd forgotten to hand in and an old taffy apple order form.

We were writing genuine research reports, according to Mrs. Bannister, and she was pretty fussy about how we did it. I decided to call Ben and see if he had the assignment sheet.

The phone rang several times before he answered.

"Whaddya doing today?" I asked.

"Not much. Just hanging around."

"Wanna work on the social studies report with me?" I asked.

"Are you kidding?" inquired Ben. "Study on a Saturday?"

Now I was embarrassed. I'd have to think fast. "Well, that Underground Railroad stuff is pretty exciting. Remember the author who came to class on Thursday? She seemed to think the old Klum house on County Line Road could have been a stop on the Underground Railroad."

"Yeah," answered Ben.

I could tell from his tone of voice I'd caught his attention. We weren't just going to read about the Underground Railroad in an encyclopedia. We were going to do "field research"—at least that's what the guest author had called it.

"I'll pick you up in five minutes," I said. The day was beginning to have possibilities.

On my way to Ben's I remembered what I'd learned about the Underground Railroad so far. It was scary to think of black people sneaking around in the middle of the night and eating plants to keep alive, just so they wouldn't have to be slaves. Sometimes the guys who were tracking them down used bloodhounds. The "stops" on the Underground Railroad were houses where the slaves hid out during the day. When it got dark, someone would take them to the next stop where they would be safe for one more night. I couldn't believe that one of the stops was close to where we lived. This was going to be the best report I'd ever written.

I should have called my mom to tell her where I was going, but I knew if she found out I was with Ben, she wouldn't be happy. I'd wait until I got an A on my report to tell her.

Ben was kicking a football around his front yard when I got there.

"Let's go," he said. "This is a great idea."

I beamed. I knew my mom would never understand why I cared about the views of a kid who had once left me lying near the train tracks with a broken leg! Maybe it didn't make sense, but Ben's opinion of me still mattered.

We headed through the tunnel under the commuter railroad tracks. The tunnel didn't seem nearly as scary to me now as it did when I first moved to town. Ben pulled out a couple of candy bars and offered me one. This was going to be a dynamite day!

I was glad for all of the jumping jacks and sit-ups I'd been doing in karate. Walking to the Klum house and back was a three-mile hike. Ben knew a shortcut through the forest preserve, but the ground was rocky and we couldn't go very fast.

"Hey, look over there," Ben said.

I turned my head just in time to see a family of deer vanish through the underbrush.

"Where did they come from?" I asked.

"Oh, they live in the preserve," Ben answered. "People in the houses around here feed them in the wintertime."

The Klum house was just across the field. From a distance it looked pretty impressive, but once we got closer, I could see the peeling paint and boarded-up windows. I got a little chill.

"Who lived there?" I asked Ben.

"My dad said that old man Klum died five years ago and hadn't paid his taxes. Now the house belongs to the county. They want to turn it into a museum or something."

We stood in what was once the front yard, over-grown with dried weeds and shrubs. The porch steps were crumbling. Just then the sun vanished behind a cloud. I shivered again.

"So what are we going to do?" Ben asked.

"Just walk around and look at it, I guess," I said.

"Aw, we've got to see the inside," said Ben. "How will we know if this really was an Underground Railroad stop if we don't go inside?"

I hesitated a moment. I really should have called my mom before I left.

"C'mon, Josh," Ben prodded. "Don't be a wimp."

My heart sank. First Tracy, now Ben. My reputation was fading fast.

"There's no way we're going to get in here," I said. "Everything is nailed up tight."

"Well, at least we can try. There's no harm in that."

We climbed the steps to the porch. I could just imagine everybody having lemonade out here after working on the farm all day. This must have been a neat place to live. Ben methodically tried the boards at each window.

"I guess you're right, Josh," he admitted. "Even Harry Houdini couldn't get in here."

"I thought Harry Houdini escaped from places," I said.

"Well, you know what I mean," Ben retorted. "Let's go around to the back."

A set of stone steps led down to what looked like a basement door. Ben pulled on it, and to our surprise it opened to reveal total darkness. A dank, musty smell greeted us.

"We can't go in here," I warned Ben. "That's trespassing. Besides, we can't see anything. It's too dark."

Ben triumphantly pulled a flashlight from his pocket. "I planned ahead," he chuckled.

If Ben put as much time into planning his homework as he did other stuff, he'd be a straight-A student. I would never have thought to bring a flashlight along. Of course, I hadn't been planning on actually going into the house either.

"I wonder why this door is open," Ben asked. "This is too easy."

Maybe Ben was right, and I was a wimp. I peered in from the top of the stairs. I didn't want to go down there. The way my life was going this year, I'd probably break my other leg and Ben would desert me again.

He shone the flashlight into the blackness. "We don't have to go all the way in," he said. "Since the door was open, we're not really doing anything wrong. This is research! Don't be a chicken."

Ben knew my "Achilles heel." I learned about that from my Aunt Kathy who teaches at a university. Your Achilles heel is some place where you're weak and somebody can get to you. It's from Greek mythology, I think.

I didn't want anybody to think I was afraid, especially Ben. I descended the stone steps into the inky unknown. Ben played the flashlight about the room. It had a dirt floor, just like my basement. Over in a far corner there was a huge hole in the wall. It looked like a cave or tunnel. Ben pointed the flashlight to the other side. A cot stood against the wall and next to it a tattered shopping bag.

"I wonder what that is," he said. "Let's look."

I reached out and pulled him back. "C'mon," I said. "We were just gonna look, not really go inside."

"But this is great," he enthused. "I can't believe we actually got in here. You go back if you want. I'm gonna check this out."

The temptation was too great. I followed Ben across the uneven dirt floor. There was a dirty pillow and torn blanket on the cot.

"It looks like somebody's been sleeping here," I said.

"You're right," Ben answered. "Look, there's a flashlight under the blanket. Maybe it's one of those homeless people you hear about on TV."

"We'd better get outta here," I said. I could just imagine someone interrupting our investigation. I'd seen pictures of those homeless people. They were scary.

"Okay," said Ben, "but we've gotta come back another time. This is a terrific place. Just look at that tunnel over there. I wonder where it goes."

We climbed the steps, and Ben pulled the creaking door back into place. We set across the field back to town.

Monday was pizza day in the cafeteria. That was the good news. The bad news was that they usually served some pale, tasteless vegetable along with it. Today it was peas. And that meant that the trouble-makers were trying to shoot them through their straws to see what would happen. The same thing always did. Mrs. Borthistle, the gym teacher who also supervised lunch, swooped down from out of nowhere and banished the culprits to the cleanup table.

Ben Anderson spent a lot of time at the cleanup table. Maybe he liked pushing the mop around the gym after the rest of us went out to play. Or maybe getting a reaction out of Mrs. Borthistle was worth it. But now I couldn't talk to him about our plans for after school. If we hurried we'd have time to go back to the Klum house before I had to go to karate.

"How was your weekend?" Wendell asked, as we threw our Styrofoam trays into the bin. We recycled everything at Jefferson School.

I wasn't sure how to respond. Telling Wendell something was a lot like telling my mom. He was so sensible and always did the right thing. I knew I'd end up getting a lecture if I told him the truth. I decided to play it cool.

"Oh, I did a little work on my Underground Railroad report," I replied. I hoped he wouldn't dig deeper.

"We had a good time at my grandma's place," said Wendell. "We had a flat tire on the expressway, and my dad and I had to change it. It was great."

He started telling me all the details, but I was thinking that my dad and I had never changed a tire together. What would happen if Mom and I got one when we were driving? I wondered if she could change a flat.

"Wanna shoot some baskets?" I asked. I saw Mrs. Ravenswood, the fourth-grade teacher, playing with the kids in her class.

"Naw," said Wendell. "Let's pick up some trash." Jefferson School is big on the environment. Not only do they recycle, but they are always beautifying the playground. Kids who want to pick up papers and junk on the playground can get gloves and bags and do cleanup during lunch hour. The Student Council gives prizes to the kids who pick up the most.

"I don't feel like it," I said. "You go ahead."

Now I was standing all alone in the middle of the blacktop. I tried to look inconspicuous. There's nothing worse than being alone at lunch recess, at least in my opinion. But someone was coming toward me. It was Tracy Kendall.

"Hi, Josh," she said.

I didn't know whether to answer or run the other way. It seemed different to talk to her out here.

"Are you going to Awana tomorrow night?" she asked.

"Sure," I said.

"Do you like it?" she asked.

"Oh, yeah." I wanted to tell her that since I'd accepted Christ as my Savior, Awana meant more to me than just a bunch of games. I was really into reading the Bible and learning what it meant to be a Christian. But somehow I just couldn't figure out how to say all that to Tracy.

"Bye," she said. I wondered if she'd ever talk to me again.

The bell rang and Mrs. Bannister's class lined up in our assigned spot. Trevor was standing right behind me. I wondered what he'd been doing during recess. Did he have anybody to play with?

Mrs. Bannister led us into the classroom, and we got quiet right away because we wanted her to begin reading aloud. She'd started a new book about this guy named Dies Drear who was an abolitionist. That meant he was against slavery. His house had been a station on the Underground Railroad. The book was called *The House of Dies Drear*.

Mrs. Bannister didn't read aloud like my old teacher who put everyone to sleep. Mrs. Bannister made us all forget that we were at Jefferson School. For the twenty minutes she read, it was like being someplace else.

Her voice dropped to almost a whisper as she read about the "dark, isolated look" of Dies Drear's house. It sounded like the Klum house. I sure wanted to see that place again after hearing Mrs. Bannister read aloud. I wanted to read the book for myself, too.

Not only was Monday pizza day, but we had gym and music in the afternoon too. It was almost like being on vacation. We're learning how to play volleyball in gym and how to play the recorder in music. Mrs. Bannister says we're going to be well rounded when we graduate from Jefferson.

When the bell rang at 3:00, Ben waved me over to his desk. "Can we do it?" he asked.

Without a minute's hesitation, I said yes. If that boy Thomas could do it, so could I. I was ready for adventure.

"Let's grab a snack at my house," I said. "I'll pick up a flashlight, too."

The walk to the Klum house seemed shorter this time. Ben and I talked the whole way about what we wanted to do. At the top of the list was exploring that hole in the wall. If the house had been a station on the Underground Railroad like our guest author Glennette Turner thought, that would be a great spot to hide people.

The days were getting shorter now, and the sky was dark and overcast. It even looked a little like snow. I was glad my winter jacket still fit. It made me worry, though, that I hadn't grown much since last winter. I hoped I wasn't going to be short like Dad.

"There it is," said Ben. "I wonder if there'll be anybody there."

The house looked even gloomier than it had before. I was thinking about the house of Dies Drear. I was also thinking about the owner of the cot and the shopping bag. I'd taken for granted that the person only slept there at night. What would we do if someone was there now?

Ben was whistling. I didn't know if that meant he was happy or just nervous. "Let's knock on the door first," he suggested.

"Do you think someone's just going to answer the door like they're expecting company for tea?" I asked sarcastically.

"We could shout a warning," said Ben. "That would let him know we're here."

"How do you know it's a he?" I asked.

"You don't think some girl would sleep down in

36

that basement, do you?" he challenged me.

"I bet Tracy Kendall would," I said. "Or Mrs. Ravenswood. They're both cool."

"Yeah, I noticed you talking to Tracy today on the playground," said Ben. "Is she your girlfriend?"

I stuttered a little when I answered. "N-n-no, not really. She just goes to my church."

"Since when have you been going to church?" asked Ben. "You don't seem the type."

Now was my chance to do what the minister called witnessing. Witnessing is when you tell someone what you believe so they can decide if they want to believe the same thing. Wendell witnessed to me when I first moved into town. So did Sonny. But I didn't have the nerve to do it yet.

Besides, how would it look to witness to Ben when I was here doing something I shouldn't be doing? Come to think of it, I guessed maybe when you were doing something you weren't supposed to be doing, that was sin. That's what the Bible calls all the bad things people do. When you decide to be a Christian, your sins are forgiven. I guessed poking around in the basement of the Klum house wasn't really like killing somebody or stealing money, so maybe it wasn't sin. It was all very confusing sometimes.

"I just go to church once in a while," I said. Now I really had sinned. I'd told a lie. I went to church every Sunday, and I also went to Awana on Tuesdays.

Why couldn't I just tell Ben straight out? This trip was beginning to cause me a whole lot of trouble.

Ben reached out and pounded on the basement door. "Hey, in there, it's Ben Anderson and Joshua McIntire. We're coming in, ready or not."

He pushed the door, and we both pointed our flashlights into the darkness. There was a stirring from across the room, and a faint voice responded to our shouts.

"Don't shoot. I'll leave. Don't shoot."

Ben and I looked at each other in alarm. Who said anything about shooting? We almost stumbled over each other backing up the steps and running across the yard. But we couldn't help but look back.

The creature who emerged from the darkness rubbing his eyes looked like a main character in *Beauty and the Beast*—and he wasn't the princess. He was wearing layers of torn clothing and had a shaggy beard. We didn't wait for introductions.

"Hey, wait," the man called. "Come back." Then he collapsed at the top of the stairs.

"Oh, great," said Ben. "Now what do we do?"

I remembered the time Ben had left me with a broken leg. He was probably thinking of doing the same thing now.

"We can't leave him," I said. "He really looks sick."

"But if we tell somebody, we'll get into trouble," Ben reasoned.

"I know," I said, "but we can do what they always do on TV. Make an anonymous phone call."

"Yeah," said Ben. "You can do it."

Ben was a great guy. Always willing to let his friends go first.

"We'd better hurry," I said. "He didn't look real good."

"We can use the phone booth down by the commuter station," Ben suggested. "You can just dial 911."

We ran as fast as we could back to town. I was breathing hard, but Ben looked like he was having a heart attack. My karate conditioning was coming in handy.

I stepped into the phone booth. My hands were shaking as I punched the numbers. I wondered if the police in Grandville could trace calls to phone booths like they did in the movies.

A crisp voice answered after only one ring. "This is 911 Emergency for Grandville. Is this an emergency?"

What a dumb question, I thought. *Why would I be dialing 911 if it weren't?* I tried to keep my voice from quavering.

"There's a man who's hurt out at the old Klum house," I reported.

"And who are you?" the crisp voice asked.

That was when I hung up the receiver and grabbed Ben.

"Let's get outta here," I said, and we darted into the tunnel under the train tracks. Its darkness was welcoming now. I just wanted to get home and think about what had happened. Whenever I did something with Ben, it always turned into trouble with a capital T.

I was glad that Mom wasn't back from work when I got home. She was good at figuring out when something was bothering me, and she would have wormed it out of me. I grabbed a banana from the fruit bowl and started shoving it into my mouth while I changed into my *gi*. That's the uniform I wear for karate. It's supposed to be white, but somehow after a couple of washings, the color changed to a dingy gray. Mom says the water in Grandville is impossible. Only Master Lee's uniform stays white. I think he puts on a new one every week.

While I was changing, the phone rang—Mom calling to check up on me.

"Joshua, where have you been?" she asked frantically. "I've been calling for the past half hour."

I wished she wouldn't worry so much. "Ben and I were working on our social studies report," I said. That was the truth.

"Well, I'm going to be a little late again. Mr.

Terpstra is finishing up a project, and I can use the overtime, " she said apologetically.

"That's okay, Mom," I said. "I'll just make a sandwich and walk to karate."

"I'm glad you're learning to be so responsible," she said. "I think maybe you're really growing up."

I groaned inside. If she only knew.

"I'll pick you up at Master Lee's at seven o'clock sharp," she said. "Bye. I love you."

Even though I'd only had a banana and a candy bar since lunch, I wasn't feeling that hungry. I kept thinking about that ragged looking man at the Klum house. I wondered if he was okay. Maybe I'd skip dinner tonight.

Just then I remembered my yellow belt test. Tonight was practice, and next week I'd have to break one of those wooden boards if I wanted to pass. I wasn't sure I could do it.

The minute I got to karate I started the warm-up exercises. I wasn't the newest student anymore, and that was a good feeling. There was even a high schooler who didn't know as much as I did. He jiggled in all the wrong places and was really out of shape. After warm-up I practiced the routines for my belt test.

"What is wrong tonight, young Joshua?" asked Master Lee. "Karate requires concentration and relaxation."

How could I concentrate and relax at the same time? My life was too complicated.

"Let's try it again," he said patiently. His voice was soft and soothing, and I found myself forgetting about everything but the movement of my arms and legs.

I didn't see my mom slip in the front door. Master Lee bowed to her, and she bowed in return. All that bowing was a little embarrassing, but Master Lee insisted on it.

Mom and I drove home in silence. She must have been tired, and I was thinking about all the stuff I hadn't told her—about dad's package, the Klum house, and especially that poor man.

Mom was in the kitchen reading the newspaper when I got up.

"Look at these headlines," she said. " 'Homeless Man Near Death from Malnutrition.' "

I swallowed hard and walked over to the refrigerator so she couldn't see my face. She continued to read aloud.

Area officials are looking for a young boy or girl who phoned in the tip that may have saved a homeless man's death from malnutrition. The police received an anonymous phone call at about 5:00 p.m. Monday notifying them of the man's collapse on the premises of the Klum homestead on County Line Road. The man, not yet identified by police, had apparently been living in the basement of the home. Hospital officials report that the man, probably age 60 or 70, is resting comfortably in intensive care where he has been receiving intravenous feedings. Police are waiting for him to regain consciousness so they can question him about his identity and any relationship he may have had to the anonymous caller. Anyone with information is asked to call the Grandville Police Department.

Mom laid the newspaper down and carried her dishes to the sink. "I'll be home on time tonight. What do you want for dinner?"

I'd regained my composure. "Let's have hamburgers," I said.

"Good idea. Do you want to invite Wendell?" she asked. "You have Awana tonight, don't you?"

Feeling the way I did, I wasn't sure I wanted to see Wendell. I shook my head. "I'll have homework to do," I said.

"Okay. See you this afternoon," she called cheerily as she went out the back door.

I was deep in thought when I suddenly realized that the phone was ringing.

"Hey, Josh, did you see the paper?" It was Ben.

"Yeah," I answered.

"Isn't it neat?" he asked.

Ben never seemed to be upset by trouble. In fact, he thrived on it. I wondered if he'd ever heard of sin.

"Are you going to turn yourself in?" he asked.

"That would really be neat. You could be a hero. I wish I'd called."

What I wished is that I'd done the right thing and told Ben to forget it when this whole thing started. But now it was too late. How was I going to get out of this mess?

By the time Thursday afternoon rolled around, I couldn't wait to get to Studebaker's Leather Emporium. I had a part-time job there sweeping the floor and helping Sonny straighten skins and fold patterns. In addition to being able to make just about anything from leather, Sonny was my good friend. If it weren't for Sonny, I wouldn't be taking karate or be a Christian. Today I hoped we'd have some time to talk. I really needed some advice.

"Josh, my man. How's it going?" Sonny called from the back of the shop.

"Okay," I said, but he must have detected the note of dejection in my voice.

"You don't sound okay; what's the deal?" He came quickly to the counter where I was standing.

I knew if I started talking, I'd cry. It seemed like I was always crying in front of Sonny. I hoped he wouldn't think I was a wimp too. But I couldn't hold it in any longer. I was mad at my dad, mad at myself for being such a jerk, and mad at Ben for messing me up again.

I was a Christian now. Why couldn't I do the right thing? Wendell never seemed to have any trouble. He was perfect as far as I could tell.

"Let's have a Coke and talk about it," Sonny said. He went to the back room to get the soft drinks, and that gave me the chance I needed to clear my throat and my eyes.

"Things aren't going too good," I said. I started babbling, and everything got mixed up.

"Now wait a minute," Sonny said. "What does the Underground Railroad have to do with sin?"

I started over again and told him about the package from Dad, the social studies assignment, and what Ben and I had done.

"Wow," he said, when I'd finished. "For a kid, you sure do get into some messes. Know what I'd recommend?"

My chin dropped to my chest, and I shook my head dejectedly.

"Joshua, I'm surprised at you. What always works when you've got a problem you don't know how to solve?"

"Karate and prayer?" I asked.

"Well, in this case, I think we'd better move right to prayer," he answered.

"I don't know," I said. "Prayer never seems to get me what I want. Like my mom and dad getting back together again."

46

"Aha," said Sonny. "That's where you're making a very critical error in judgment."

I wished he wouldn't use so many big words. "What do you mean?" I asked.

"Prayer," said Sonny, "is not for getting what you want. It's for getting what you need. God provides for our needs, not our wants."

"I don't get it," I said.

"Well, let me give you an example. When I first opened up this shop, I wanted lots of money. So I prayed for lots of customers. I got a little upset with God when people didn't start pouring through my doors. I was a new Christian then, like you are now," he explained. "I didn't understand that just because I wanted something and prayed for it, that didn't mean God would necessarily give it to me. God knew what I needed. I've never starved; actually I've done pretty well. But that only happened when I stopped telling God what to do."

It was obvious that I had a lot to learn about prayer. But talking to Sonny made me feel a lot better.

"I think maybe we'd better ask God for some advice here," said Sonny.

"I already know what I should do," I replied.

"Oh, He's been talking to you already," Sonny said with a laugh. "Let's make sure we don't miss anything important."

We bowed our heads and each whispered a brief prayer.

"Now tell me what you think God wants you to do," he said.

"First off, I need to talk to my mom," I told him. "Then I need to call the police. And then I need to tell Ben Anderson a thing or two."

He nodded and smiled at me. "You've got your work cut out for you. Just be patient with Ben."

"Sonny," I said, "there's one more thing I don't understand. How come Wendell never seems to have any problems with this thing called sin?"

"Something I've learned," said Sonny, "is that you can't always tell what's going on in another person's life. Wendell's temptations—that's what it's called when somebody has a hard time doing the right thing—might be totally different from yours. But everybody is sinful. Don't ever forget that. We all need God's forgiveness every day."

That made me feel a little better . . . though I had a hard time believing that God could love me as much as He loved Wendell when I kept messing things up all the time.

Telling the whole story to Sonny had made me feel a lot better. Or maybe it was talking to God about it that had done it. At any rate, I knew what I was going to do now. First I had to tell Mom, who'd be home any minute.

I poured myself a glass of milk and stirred in some chocolate syrup. It always surprised me when the milk suddenly changed from white to brown. It was a mystery how that happened. That's the way I felt sometimes—one minute light and the next minute dark. I squirted in some more syrup to see how dark I could get it.

I heard the car pull up in the driveway, and I quickly swallowed the last of my chocolate milk. I should have started dinner.

"C'mon, Josh, let's go," Mom called from the front door.

"Where are we going?" I shouted. "I thought we were having hamburgers for supper."

"We're doing Chinese tonight," she answered.

I wondered what the occasion was. We didn't eat out that often. The last time had been when I'd taken Mom to McDonald's with my first earnings from Sonny. I grabbed my jacket, turned out the light, and went racing through the house before she changed her mind.

I climbed into our car. It was the one we'd picked out with Dad when we were a family. The bright blue was his favorite color. One of his friends had painted racing stripes on the side. I wondered if he missed his car as much as I missed him.

"So, Joshua McIntire," Mom began, "what's happening in your life?"

I couldn't tell if she was kidding or serious. Did she know something was happening in my life? Was that the real reason we were going out for dinner?

"I do have some things to tell you, Mom, but could we wait until we get there?"

"Sure, Joshua," she said. "No problem."

"How was your day?" I asked.

"Actually, pretty good," she said. "Mr. Terpstra and I finished the special project so I won't have to work this weekend. The overtime I get for it will give us a good start on Christmas shopping. And I'm having dinner with the handsomest man I know," she finished. "So my day's been pretty good."

I was glad she was in a good mood. After I laid all

50

my problems on her, I wasn't sure she would still think I was the handsomest man she knew. After all, she had this saying that "handsome is as handsome does." And I'd done some pretty stupid things lately.

The Chinese restaurant was next to Master Lee's karate school. Funny I'd never noticed it before. A solitary man was seated at a table near the back. He glanced our way and then went back to devouring a huge plate of rice.

We picked out a booth. The Chinese restaurant in Woodview had the same red plastic seats. I wondered if the same person owned them.

Mom didn't waste any time. She gave me the third degree as soon as we sat down.

"So, Joshua, what's the big mystery? What do you have to tell me?" She looked at me with her wide smile and bright blue eyes. My mom was really pretty.

"Can we wait until we order?" I asked.

"Are you avoiding telling me something, Joshua?" she probed.

"Nah, Mom. I'm just hungry."

The menu brought back lots of memories. We always ordered Chinese food from a place near Dad's auto parts store. He'd pick it up on his way home from work.

"Chop suey for me," I told the waiter. That was Dad's favorite.

Now I was ready to talk. I'd had a chance to rehearse it all with Sonny so when I told it this time, I wouldn't get mixed up.

Mom's eyes got wide when I told her about the package and the letter from Dad.

"Oh, Josh. I'm so sorry that you feel bad. I wish I could kiss your 'owie' and make it better like I used to when you were little."

"That's not all, Mom," I added. "There's some more."

"What, Joshua?" Now the tone in her voice changed. She got a worried look on her face.

I felt bad, but I had to go on. I told her about going to the Klum house with Ben.

"Oh, Josh, you know you're not supposed to go places without checking with me first," she said softly. Then she got an alarmed look on her face. "Wasn't the Klum place where they found that homeless man?"

I nodded.

"Josh!" She almost shouted my name, and the waiter glanced our way. She quickly covered her mouth with her hand as if to keep in what she was going to say next. "Were you there?" she asked.

I nodded ever so slightly. "Uh huh."

"Were you the boy who called the police?"

I nodded again.

"Why didn't you give your name?" she wondered.

"I don't know. I thought I'd get into trouble, I guess."

"What were you doing there?" she asked.

"Ben and I were working on our social studies report."

"What in the world does social studies have to do with the Klum house?"

I explained all about the Underground Railroad and the author and the cave we thought was in the basement.

"How do you know there's a cave in the basement?" she asked. "You weren't actually *in* that house, were you?"

I nodded again.

"Oh, Joshua," she said sadly. She was almost crying now. "Where do you get these ideas?"

I didn't want to lay all of the blame on Ben, but if I hadn't been hanging around with him none of this would have happened. Or would it?

"I think you need to call the police, Josh. They've been trying to find the boy who made the call. If you get in trouble for being in that house, you'll just have to take the consequences."

I knew all about consequences. I'd had plenty of them since we moved to Grandville.

The waiter put the steaming dishes of food on the table. Mom was having sweet and sour pork. In spite of my troubles, for the first time in two days I was actually hungry. Telling Mom made me feel better. I started shoveling the food in.

"Are you inhaling that chop suey, Joshua?" Mom teased. "I've never seen anything disappear so fast in my life."

After we'd finished, Mom sipped her tea from her miniature cup. We unwrapped our fortune cookies. Mine said, "Your life will be filled with adventure and excitement." It was a good thing I didn't believe in fortune cookies, or I would have been worried. I sure didn't need any more adventure or excitement.

As we walked to the car, I looked in Master Lee's window. I could see someone from Jefferson who had just started lessons. I remembered when I was brand new. Now I was almost ready for my first belt test.

"I think you'd better call the police as soon as we get home," Mom said as we were driving down Main Street.

"Aw, can't I wait until tomorrow?" I begged.

"The sooner the better, Josh," she said sternly. "Let's get it over with."

"Do I call 911?" I wondered.

"I don't think this is exactly an emergency," she said. "We'll look up the regular number in the phone book."

Neither of us said anything the rest of the way home. While Mom locked up the car, I stood on the front porch waiting for her. I could hear the phone ringing, but my key was in my book bag. It was probably Wendell. We'd hardly talked to each other lately. I needed to tell him what was going on too.

The phone kept ringing. The caller was persistent. As soon as Mom turned the key, I pushed through the door. I needn't have worried. The phone was still ringing.

I was breathless when I picked it up. "Hello, this is the McIntire residence."

"Don't you ever stay home?" a voice said. My heart jumped. It was Dad.

"Oh, we went out for dinner," I said.

"Did you get my package?" he asked.

"Yeah," I said.

"Have you put it together yet?"

"N-n-no," I stammered. "I've been pretty busy."

"Well, I hope you like it," Dad replied.

"It's great, Dad. Thanks." At least I remembered my manners.

"Can I talk to your mom?" he asked. My heart leapt. Maybe my prayers were going to be answered right here and now.

"Sure," I said.

"Dad wants to talk to you," I said. I hoped my excitement wasn't too obvious.

Mom gave me a funny look and took the receiver from my hand.

She put it to her ear and in a voice I could hardly

hear said, "Hello, Jerry." I'd almost forgotten my dad's name, it had been so long since I'd heard anybody say it.

She stood there not saying anything. He was doing all the talking. She was just murmuring "hmm" and "okay."

"Well, I'm not sure," she said.

I just knew he was asking if he could come back home. Why wasn't she sure? This was dumb.

"We haven't made any plans yet," she said.

That was dumb too. What plans would interfere with his coming back?

"Let me ask him," she said. She covered the receiver with her hand and motioned me toward her.

"Your father wants you to come visit him for Thanksgiving," she said. "He's found an apartment in Northfield and is working at an auto parts store there."

My face fell. He didn't want to come back home.

"Don't you want to go?" she asked.

I didn't know what I wanted. This wasn't what I was expecting.

"You don't have to make up your mind now," she said. "We can call him back." She sounded as though she weren't sure either.

But I was afraid if I didn't say yes now that Dad would change his mind. I blurted it out before I knew what I was saying.

"No, Mom. I don't need to think about it. I'll go." I had no idea where Northfield was.

She got a strange look on her face as she uncovered the receiver.

"Jerry, Joshua says he'll come, but I have no idea how he'll get there. Northfield is three hundred miles from here, and the car is not up for that kind of a trip."

She grew silent again, and I could tell that Dad was giving her one of his big explanations. He was always good at big explanations.

"Oh, I don't know if that's practical," she said.

I wondered what they were talking about now.

"Well, if you can send the money, I might consider it," she said. "But Joshua seems to find trouble wherever he goes lately. I'm not sure I'd trust him on a three-hundred-mile bus ride."

I couldn't believe what I was hearing. I jumped up and down, waving my arms and nodding my head. She was actually considering letting me go on a three-hundred-mile bus ride to see my dad for Thanksgiving. Wow! Wait until I told Wendell about this.

Mom hung up the phone slowly. "Now, nothing's been decided, Joshua. I've got to think about this for a day or two. Three hundred miles is a long way for a ten-year-old boy."

"I'll be good, Mom. Honest, I will. I promise."

Then it hit me. If I went to visit Dad for Thanksgiving, Mom would be all by herself. I couldn't do that.

"I know what you're thinking, Joshua. If I decide you can go, I'll go to Aunt Kathy's for Thanksgiving. She's been after me to visit her for months."

"Are you sure, Mom?" I asked.

"I'm sure," she said. "As a matter of fact, I think you need to see your father. I'll just have to trust that you've learned some lessons these past few days. You need to think about what you do before you do it."

"Does that mean I can go?"

"It does," she said.

"Thank you, thank you, thank you." I twirled around the room shouting my thanks at the top of my lungs.

"Before you get too excited, you've got some business to take care of, don't you?" she asked.

Suddenly I was brought back to reality. I had to call the police and tell them I'd made that emergency call. Mom looked up the number for me and we practiced together what I should say.

The phone call wasn't as traumatic as I thought it would be. The officer who took the information said he'd stop by school tomorrow to see me. He said they were a little shorthanded at the station and he couldn't spare anybody tonight.

I was exhausted. Talk about going from dark to

light. My mind was whirling with all that had happened.

I gave my mom a big hug. I could see the tears forming in her eyes.

"Don't worry, Mom. I'll be all right," I assured her.

"It's not you I'm worried about, Joshua," she said.

I wondered what she meant by that, but I was too tired to think about it.

"Good night, Mom. Sleep tight and don't let the bedbugs bite." That was what she'd always said to me when I was little. I'd always looked under the covers very carefully to see if there really were any bed bugs.

Alone in my room, I sat on the edge of the bed slowly taking off my gym shoes. Then I remembered something. I opened my closet door and reached behind my train set to retrieve the balsa wood airplane. I was glad I hadn't broken it in half. Maybe this weekend I'd try putting it together.

As I turned out the light and slid under the covers, I thought about my conversation with Sonny that afternoon. He'd said that God provides for our needs, not our wants. I guess maybe God knew that I needed to see my dad. I decided to thank Him right away for the answer so He'd know how much I appreciated it.

Dear God, I prayed, *thank You for making my dad call. And thanks for persuading my mom to let me go on the bus. I'm sorry for the mess I've made the last few days. I should have told Mom where I was going. I shouldn't have lied to Ben about going to church. And I shouldn't have gone into the Klum house. That was trespassing. But I did call the police and helped save that man's life. Will You count that for something? Do You think I'm okay, God? I hope so. I want to be okay.*

I drifted off to sleep imagining myself behind the wheel of a Greyhound bus. Where was Northfield anyhow? Did they have bathrooms on a bus? What if I had to go in the middle of the trip?

A police car was parked in front of school when I got there Friday morning. Boy, they sure didn't waste any time. I decided to get it over with. When I walked up to the driver's side and gave a little wave to the officer, he rolled down the window.

"Can I help you, son?" he asked.

"I'm Joshua McIntire," I said. "The kid you're looking for."

The officer stuck out his hand through the window. "I'm pleased to meet you, Joshua. That's a real fine thing you did, saving that man's life."

His radio crackled. "Hang on," he said. "I want to talk to you inside the school." He mumbled something into the hand set, then stepped out of the car.

I felt like a midget next to him as we walked down the hall to the office. I wasn't sure what was coming next.

Mrs. Raymond, the principal, was behind the counter.

"Good morning, Officer Spencer," she said in her usual cheery voice. Then she spied me, and the look on her face changed. "Joshua, what are you doing in here so early? The bell doesn't ring for another ten minutes."

"He's with me, ma'am," said the officer.

Then she really got a look on her face. Mrs. Raymond was a lot happier than my principal in Woodview, but she didn't like it at all when her students got in trouble with the law.

"Joshua?" she questioned. "Are you in trouble?"

"Oh, no, ma'am," explained Officer Spencer. "To the contrary. Joshua is a hero."

Her bright smile returned. "Come into my office and tell me all about it," she said.

This could have been really terrific—but Officer Spencer and Mrs. Raymond didn't know the whole story. And when they did, I wasn't sure they would still be smiling.

We sat down in Mrs. Raymond's office. It was getting to be a familiar place.

"So," she said, "Josh is a hero, is he?"

Officer Spencer started to tell her about the homeless man, but she stopped him in mid-sentence. "I read about that in the paper," she said. "Joshua, are you the boy who called 911?"

I nodded. Then she asked the question I'd been waiting for.

"What were you doing way out at the Klum house, Joshua? That's a long way from your house, isn't it?"

I nodded again. Then I took a deep breath and told my story for the third time. They listened without interrupting as I explained what happened. I told them about the Underground Railroad project, Ben, and the open door.

"You've certainly made the right decision in telling us everything, Joshua," said Mrs. Raymond. "I'm proud of your honesty. I wish you'd had better judgment in the first place, but in this case, it looks as though it worked out for the best."

"We wanted to give you a police department commendation," said Officer Spencer, "but I'm not sure how the chief will feel when he hears you were trespassing."

At this point, I didn't really care. I just wanted the whole thing to be over. I knew that Ben would probably get it from Mrs. Raymond, and I was worried about that. I didn't want him to be mad at me.

"Why don't you go down to class, Josh?" said Mrs. Raymond. "I want to talk to Officer Spencer."

I left her office and walked slowly down the hall. In my old school, I didn't even know what the inside of the principal's office looked like. Here I was practically on a first-name basis with Mrs. Raymond.

Mrs. Bannister was bringing the class in, and Ben waved at me.

"Hey, Josh," he called, "I've got something really neat to show you."

"Later, Ben," said Mrs. Bannister. "We've got work to do now."

I didn't have a chance to talk to Ben until lunch recess.

"C'mon over here," he motioned, pointing to a small grove of trees. He pulled me behind one of them and reached into his pocket. "Look what I found."

He had some old bones, a piece of rusty pulley, and a brass safety pin. It looked like junk to me.

"What's the big deal?" I asked.

"You don't get it, do you?" he grumbled impatiently. "I found this stuff in the Klum house. It's proof that somebody used that cave to hide in."

"You went back there?" I said. "After what happened?"

"Yeah," he said. "Since that old guy was gone, I had the place all to myself."

Ben was unbelievable!

"Weren't you scared?" I asked.

"Nah," he said. "I brought my boombox along and played it real loud."

"If that stuff is really from the Underground Railroad, you can't keep it," I said, pointing to what Ben had in his hand. "It doesn't belong to you."

"Finders, keepers," he said boastfully.

"But you know what the author Mrs. Turner said about the importance of artifacts. She said they're very valuable."

"If I don't tell, nobody'll ever know."

I couldn't believe what a sneak Ben was being.

"Well, the police know you were there," I said. The words slipped out before I could help it.

His eyes got big and round. "You ratted on me," he said accusingly.

"I had to," I said. "I told my mom about the homeless man and she made me tell the police."

"You are such a wimp, McIntire!" he shouted. "You're gonna pay for this."

Ben stomped off and left me standing alone in the grove of trees. No matter what I did, I couldn't make everybody happy.

School dragged by. Ben didn't look at me for the rest of the day.

After school Wendell caught up with me.

"What's wrong with you lately, Josh?" he asked. "You never wanna do anything with me. I thought we were friends." His voice was a little sad.

Now even Wendell was upset. Before this thing was over, nobody would like me.

"I gotta go to work, Wen," I said. "I'm not mad, honest I'm not."

I made a beeline for the leather shop. Maybe Sonny could help me figure things out again.

Sonny's boombox was playing one of the songs his group, "The King's Messengers," had recorded. It was one of my favorites, a song about God's love being endless as the ocean. I'd never seen the ocean, but I could just imagine it going on forever and ever.

"How's it going today, buddy?" Sonny asked.

"So-so," I answered. "I did the stuff we talked about and told everybody about being at the Klum house. I think that's going to work out okay."

"That's great news," he said. "So, why so glum?"

"Everybody's mad at me," I said. "Ben is mad 'cause I ratted on him. Wendell is mad 'cause I haven't had any time to even talk to him lately. I'm in a mess again."

"I'm going to make a sign for you to hang up in your room," said Sonny. "It's going to say, 'When all else fails, pray!' "

That's when I remembered my first real answer to prayer. "My dad called last night and invited me to spend Thanksgiving," I said. Suddenly I felt better. I told Sonny all about it while I swept the floor. By the time I'd finished my other chores, I was smiling again.

Mrs. Bannister gave us time to work on our social studies reports on Monday afternoon. I went down to the library to check out an encyclopedia. There wasn't much in the *World Book*, but it told me some stuff I didn't know, such as that the hiding places were called "stations" and the people who helped the runaways were called "conductors."

I took notes on some 3" x 5" cards so Mrs. Bannister would be able to tell I wasn't copying straight from the encyclopedia. I kept thinking about the basement in the Klum house. If the stuff that Ben found was authentic, then maybe it had been a stop on the Underground. I could just imagine somebody crawling back into that hole in the wall and trying to be quiet for a whole day. I sure couldn't do that.

"Are you sleeping?" Somebody touched my arm and I jumped.

"No," I blurted out, embarrassed at being caught in my daydreams.

It was Trevor. "What are you doing?" he asked.

"I'm working on my Underground Railroad report," I said.

"You were sleeping," Trevor said again, with certainty in his voice.

I suddenly remembered that Mrs. Bannister had asked me to help Trevor with his report. Maybe now was a good time to do that.

I wasn't really sure how you helped somebody with a report, but I thought I'd start by asking Trevor what he thought the Underground Railroad was.

"It's a train that runs under the ground," he said.

"That's what I thought before too," I explained. "But it isn't a train and it isn't underground."

Trevor looked puzzled. I tried to think of a good way to explain this so he would understand.

"Have you ever played hide-and-seek?" I asked.

Trevor nodded.

"Well, you know how you hide from somebody so they can't find you?"

Trevor nodded again. I was on a roll.

"Well, the Underground Railroad was a bunch of houses where black people hid when they were running away from being slaves."

"What's a slave?" Trevor asked. This was getting more complicated.

"A slave is somebody who belongs to somebody else and has to work for them all the time," I explained.

"Slaves aren't allowed anymore."

"Where are the trains?" Trevor asked with a puzzled look on his face.

"I already told you that," I said impatiently. "There aren't any trains."

Trevor looked hurt, and I was immediately sorry I'd been cross.

"I'm sorry, Trev," I apologized. "I'm just having a bad day."

"Are you sad?" he asked in his shy, quiet voice.

"Yeah, I guess so," I said. Before I knew it, he reached out and hugged me. I was glad there wasn't anybody looking.

"You're my friend," he said. "I don't want you to be sad." He gave me that great big smile of his.

"You're my friend too," I replied. "But you know what, Trevor? Guys don't hug each other at school. They shake hands." I demonstrated. "Or sometimes they give each other high fives."

"What's a high five?" Trevor asked.

I grabbed his right wrist with my left and held it up in the air. His hand fell limp.

"Hold your hand up straight," I said.

I slapped his hand with my right hand. The clap resounded in the near-empty library.

"That's a high five," I said. "Guys do that to other guys when they like them."

He smiled shyly and tentatively held up his right

hand. I held mine up and we high-fived again.

"We'd better get back to class," I said. "Mrs. Bannister will think we got lost."

The good feeling I had after my library encounter with Trevor lasted all the way till dinnertime. It also helped that we were having meatballs with noodles. I ate five of them, which was close to my record of eight at one meal.

"Why are you in such a good mood?" Mom asked.

I told her about Trevor.

"Josh, you're like the little girl with the curl."

"Huh?" I said.

"Don't you remember that poem from your nursery rhyme book?" She recited it for me. "There was a little girl who had a little curl, right in the middle of her forehead. When she was good, she was very, very good. And when she was bad, she was horrid."

"I don't get it," I said emphatically. "I'm not a little girl, and my hair isn't curly."

"You're missing the point, Josh," she said. "When you're good, you are very, very good. Like what you did for Trevor. That was a wonderful thing. Some kids would have made fun of him and laughed. You were loving and kind."

I basked in her praise, feeling ten feet tall.

"But," she went on, "when you get into trouble, you always do it first class."

"I get it," I said. "You're ambivalent about my behavior."

She smiled. "You're a little mixed up on the meaning of that word. I'm not in the least bit ambivalent. I approve of your good behavior, and I disapprove of your behavior when you don't follow the rules. But no matter what, I love you." She rumpled my hair. "Even if you don't have a curl in the middle of your forehead."

"Do you love Dad?" The words came tumbling out before I could help it.

Mom got a funny look on her face. "I'm not sure how I feel about your father anymore," she replied. "I loved him once. He's a really neat man. I just don't think he was ready for the responsibilities of marriage."

"Doesn't he like me anymore?" I asked.

"Oh, Josh, I know your father loves you very much," she said. "His leaving didn't have anything to do with you."

"Well, if he still loves me, how come it took him so long to call?"

"There are some things that are very hard to explain," she said. "That's why I'm going to let you take the bus to Northfield. I think you and your dad need to talk to each other."

"Do you think I can persuade him to come back?" I asked.

"I wouldn't try that, Joshua," she said.

"Why not?" I said. "I bet I could do it. He always said that I should be a lawyer when I grew up."

"Well," she said slowly, "you might be able to convince him, but what about me?"

I looked at her in dismay. "I thought you were upset when Dad left," I said accusingly. "You cried all the time, didn't you?"

"You're right, Joshua. I was upset. But that was nine months ago. Things have changed."

"What things have changed?" I shouted. My earlier good feelings had vanished.

She patted me on the arm. "Calm down, Joshua, and just listen to me."

"I don't want to listen," I said. "Maybe it was your fault that Dad left in the first place." My voice sounded harsh and accusing.

The tears welled up in her eyes, and I was immediately sorry for what I'd said.

"Aw, Mom. I didn't mean that."

"We should have talked about this a long time ago," she said. "I just couldn't figure out a way to do it."

"What do you mean?" I asked.

"When your father first left," she explained, "I was devastated. But I'm learning to stand on my own two feet now," she said.

"You've always stood on your own feet."

"It's an expression, Joshua," she said. "It means

that I've begun to grow up and make some decisions on my own. Your father has some growing up to do, too."

I was thoroughly confused now. "But you're both grown up, Mom," I said.

"Being grown up doesn't always have to do with how old you are," she explained. "Sometimes older people do some pretty stupid things."

I was beginning to wish I'd kept my mouth shut. I was the one who'd started this whole conversation, and it wasn't turning out well at all. All along my plan had been to convince Dad to come back, and now Mom was telling me she didn't want him back. I thought grown-ups were supposed to know what to do.

I got dressed for karate with my mind in a whirl. Just when I thought I had things all figured out, it felt like somebody had taken an egg beater and whipped up my brains.

Dear God, I prayed, *now what do I do? I thought You'd answered my prayer about getting Mom and Dad back together again. Now I don't know what to pray. Could You please straighten this mess out pretty soon? And thanks for sending me a friend like Trevor. He thinks I'm great no matter what I do.*

I was leaving at noon Wednesday for Northfield. Mom had talked to Mrs. Bannister, and she said it was okay for me to miss the afternoon. Our class was helping the kindergartners cook Thanksgiving dinner. My group was in charge of cleanup, so I wasn't too disappointed about not being there.

Mom had bought my bus ticket as soon as the money from Dad came in the mail. She couldn't change her mind about letting me go now. My suitcase was packed, and she'd helped me put the balsa wood airplane in a cardboard box. I'd been working on it every spare minute. I wanted to finish it, but I was having some problems in a couple of places. Maybe Dad would be able to help me.

I tossed and turned in my bed. I thought about the verses I'd recited for Awana earlier. They talked about putting on God's armor so that you'd be safe against the tricks of Satan. I imagined myself in a suit of armor fighting off the bad guys.

I'd always pictured the devil with a pitchfork and horns, like a Halloween costume, but the verse said that "we are not fighting against people made of flesh and blood, but against persons without bodies—the evil rulers of the unseen world, those mighty satanic beings and great evil princes of darkness who rule this world; and against huge numbers of wicked spirits in the spirit world."

It sounded like Star Wars to me. But our Awana leader said that the devil tempted us in small and simple ways and that we needed to pray all the time to be kept safe. I wondered if the devil had anything to do with the trouble I kept getting into. I sure hoped he wasn't going to be along on my bus ride to Northfield. I shivered a little in the darkness. Maybe I'd better pray just in case.

Dear God, keep me safe, I prayed. *And keep my mom and dad safe too. And God, keep Wendell, and Trevor, and Tracy safe too.*

I thought about Ben. He probably needed my prayers more than anyone. The devil seemed to work overtime thinking of things for Ben to do.

Dear God, keep Ben safe too. Make the devil leave him alone so he'll stop getting into trouble.

I woke up early. The day was crisp and clear, perfect for a bus trip. Mom was picking me up at school and driving me to the bus station on her lunch hour. Over breakfast, she reviewed the rules of the trip one more time.

"Aw, Mom," I said, "I won't forget. Pay attention to what the driver says. Don't take your money out of your pocket in front of anybody. Be polite to everyone."

"Don't make the mistake of thinking you know everything, Joshua. That's what gets you into trouble," she warned.

"I'll be careful, Mom," I promised. "I'm ten years old."

"I'm putting your overnight bag and the box in my car," she said. "We'll go to the bus station right from school. I've packed you a lunch and some snacks to eat on the way." She held up a bag with my name on it.

"Aw, Mom," I said. "That looks dumb with my name written on it."

"Well, okay," she agreed. "I'll put it in another bag. See you later."

She was out the door and on her way to work.

Wendell and I always walked to school together, but I knew he wouldn't be here for another five minutes. I wandered around the house. I'd forgotten to make my bed and hang up my wet towel. Mom would be mad if I left her with a mess.

I'd just finished pulling the spread over my pillow when the doorbell rang. "Just a minute, Wen. I'll be right there," I yelled.

I looked around the living room one last time. I was feeling homesick already. This was my home now. I'd never felt that way about it before. Our house in Woodview had been home to me ever since I was a baby. Deep down I'd always thought we'd be going back there. But maybe not.

Even though the sun was shining, the air was brisk. A light coating of frost covered the housetops and lawns. Wendell and I walked fast to keep warm.

"I've never been on a bus trip before," said Wendell. "What's it like?

"I don't know," I said. "It's a new one on me, too. But my mom has given me ten thousand instructions."

"Are the seats assigned like on an airplane?" he wondered. "Do they have stewardesses?"

"I'll tell you all about it when I get back," I said. "I'll have some great stuff for my journal on Monday."

"How long will the trip take?" Wendell asked.

"It's about three hundred miles," I said, "but the bus makes some stops on the way to pick up and drop off people. I'll get there around dinner time."

"Maybe you'll sit next to a mysterious stranger," said Wendell. "That's what always happens on TV."

"I'll probably get a fat lady with a crying baby," I said. "And she'll make me hold the baby." I cringed at the prospect.

"Maybe you'll sit next to a beautiful girl," suggested

Wendell. He had a wild imagination. "She'll be running away from secret spies who are pursuing her, and she'll need protection. You'll be the hero."

"Wendell, the seat next to mine will probably be empty," I said.

Our speculations about my trip made the walk to school pass quickly. We were almost there, and I could sense that Wendell was getting serious.

"I'm glad you're getting to see your dad," said Wendell. "I hope you have a good time."

"Thanks, Wen," I said. "I do too. I'll talk to you on Monday."

I headed for the playground, and Wendell went into school. He helps out in the computer lab before school.

The clock seemed to be operating in slow motion all morning. I thought lunchtime would never come.

"Joshua," Mrs. Bannister addressed me. "Your vacation isn't beginning until noon. Let's get something done before then." She was collecting our Underground Railroad reports, and I was recopying the table of contents and bibliography. I was pretty proud of this report. I was also proud of Trevor's report. It wasn't as long as mine, but together we'd figured out what he wanted to write about and then I'd helped him with some of the words.

The bell finally rang.

"Good-bye, Joshua," said Mrs. Bannister. "Have

a wonderful Thanksgiving. We'll be eager to hear all about your trip on Monday."

I wanted to run down the hall and out the front door, but I restrained myself. I didn't need a detention.

"Hi, Mom," I said, jumping into the front seat. "I'm ready to go!"

"You don't have to look so eager to leave," she said. "I'm going to miss you."

Her comment stopped me short. I hadn't really thought about how she was feeling, I'd been so excited about my trip. "I'm sorry, Mom. I hope you have a good Thanksgiving."

She was taking the train into the city tomorrow morning and spending the day with her sister, Kathy. My aunt was an anthropology professor. She studied Egyptian stuff and wore lots of noisy jewelry.

"I'll be fine, Joshua. I just hope you have a good time. Don't be too hard on your dad. Okay?"

We pulled into the parking lot of the bus station, and I saw several big Greyhound buses parked in loading zones. I wondered which one was mine.

"Here's your ticket. Now, remember, the bus will stop about halfway there for a twenty-minute rest stop, but don't get off."

She pointed to the paper bag in the back seat. "I've packed a candy bar, two sandwiches, and a banana for lunch. I put in some homemade brownies and another banana if you get hungry later. There's a carton of milk for lunch and a can of pop to wash down the brownies."

I sure wasn't going to starve on this trip.

"Now, where's your emergency money?" she asked.

I pointed to my jeans pocket. "C'mon, Mom, I'm going to miss the bus."

We got out of the car, and I spotted my bus. It said Northfield over the front window. We walked slowly toward it. My mom bent down and gave me a quick hug. I didn't have a chance to hug her back, she stood up so quickly.

"Bye, Josh." Her voice was kind of wobbly. I sure hoped she wasn't going to get all weepy on me. This could be embarrassing.

"Bye, Mom. Don't worry. I'll be fine," I said.

"Call me the minute you get there," she reminded me. "Do you have the number written down?"

"Aw, Mom!" I said. "I can remember my own phone number."

The driver checked my ticket and loaded my overnight bag into a big compartment on the side of the bus.

"He'll put the box into the overhead rack," my mom explained.

I gave her a little wave. I wanted to play it cool in

front of the bus driver, but she spoiled it all by blowing me a kiss.

I boarded the bus and headed down the long aisle. There weren't many people, and the driver had said I could sit anywhere. I picked a seat where I could wave to Mom again. I had a lump in my throat. I watched her pull away. She had to get back to her job.

Before long other passengers arrived. There was a man in a sailor's uniform and a woman with two little kids. The kids were fighting with each other, and the mom looked frazzled. She sat across the aisle from me and plunked the kids in the seat in front of her.

"If I hear one word out of you two, I'll scream," she threatened.

This promised to be an interesting trip. I bet those two wouldn't be able to keep from fighting for more than a mile or two.

More passengers boarded the bus. A woman in a tight black dress with fingernails that must have been at least ten feet long sat in front of me. Her earrings were about five feet long and she looked like something from outer space.

I'd brought along *The House of Dies Drear.* I was reading it silently while Mrs. Bannister read it aloud. The trip would give me a chance to read ahead. But right now I was too excited to read. I couldn't wait for the bus to pull out.

"Welcome aboard, folks. I'm Dave, your driver from here to Northfield. Just a few rules and we'll be pulling out." He told us how we were supposed to stay in our seats and about the bathroom in the back of the bus. That solved that problem.

"We'll be stopping around three-thirty in Hazelton for a little stretch and will be arriving in Northfield about six-thirty. Have a pleasant trip, and thank you for traveling with Greyhound."

The engine revved up, and the bus swung out of the lot and onto the highway. I opened my sack lunch and polished off everything, including the brownies and Coke.

I must have fallen asleep, because suddenly Dave announced that we'd arrived in Hazelton. The last thing I remembered doing was smashing my Coke can and stuffing it in the bag. I felt stiff and disoriented.

"Can you help me?" a voice inquired. It was the woman across the aisle.

"I'll try," I answered. "What do you need?"

"I need some help with these kids in the restaurant," she said. "They're a handful for one person."

"I'm not supposed to leave the bus," I said.

"Oh," she said, looking disappointed. "Are you sure? I really could use a hand."

"My mom didn't want me to leave the bus—but I think she'd want me to help you."

"You can take Jeremy, and I'll take Jennifer," she instructed.

So before I really knew what had happened, I found myself in charge of Dennis the Menace's first cousin. Jeremy kicked me three times before we got off the bus. He wailed as his mother swatted him on the behind.

We found a booth near the front, and she ordered a hot fudge sundae for me.

"Would you take Jeremy to the bathroom?" the woman asked me.

"I don't wanna," Jeremy wailed. I was beginning to figure out why his mother had ordered the sundae. It was bribery, pure and simple.

I took the kicking and screaming Jeremy off to the men's room. I felt like dunking his head in the toilet to shut him up.

Back on the bus, Jeremy decided he wanted to sit next to me. First he hated me, now I was his long-lost buddy.

"Jeremy loves to have stories read to him," hinted his mother. "I'll pay you," she added in desperation.

I hesitated, but Jeremy hopped into the seat next to mine. I began to read aloud. *Frog and Toad. Bread and Jam for Frances. Small Pig. Davy and His Dog.* These were all my favorites when I was his age. This was more fun than I'd expected.

The bus rolled into Northfield right on schedule.

I'd scarcely noticed the hours passing as I read aloud to Jeremy.

"You'll make a wonderful father someday," said Jeremy's mom as she thrust a couple dollar bills into my hand.

I could hear my mother's voice echoing in my ear. "You don't have to pay me," I said.

"Nonsense," she replied. "You earned it. Tell your mother she can be proud of you." She must have been reading my mind.

I shoved the wrinkled bills into my pocket and retrieved my box from the rack.

"Bye, Joshua," said Jeremy. He waved with his pudgy hand. He was kind of a cute kid, I guess.

When I remembered where I was, my heart started pounding. Would Dad look the same? Would he remember me? Would he even be here? I said my phone number out loud just in case I needed it.

The minute I stepped from the bus I saw him. He was wearing his old University of Illinois cap. It was orange and blue and had a big Indian chief on it. He waved and I ran to him.

Should I hug him or just shake hands? I remembered what I'd told Trevor about guys hugging each other . . . but wasn't it different when one of the guys was your dad?

"Are you hungry, Josh?" Dad asked.

The last thing I'd had to eat was the hot fudge sundae in Hazelton. I nodded.

"Well, let's stop at Russell's Barbecue. It's right near my apartment."

I couldn't imagine my dad living in an apartment. I wondered who did his laundry and made his bed. Mom used to do that stuff for him when they were married.

"You're not talking very much, Josh. Cat got your tongue?" That was an expression he always used. I thought it was funny when I was little. I laughed. Maybe this would be like old times.

"Where do you work?" I asked.

"I've found a job in another auto parts store," he said. "They needed someone who really knew the stock."

"Do you like it?" I asked.

"It's okay," he said. "I'm hoping to find something better once I get settled."

He didn't explain why he'd moved here in the first place, and I didn't ask.

The barbecues were juicy, and the cole slaw and beans were good too. I was hungrier than I thought. My dad just sat back and watched me wolf down my food.

"Your table manners haven't changed much since the last time I saw you," he said with a laugh.

I had barbecue sauce dripping off my chin.

"So, are you mad at your old dad for not calling much?" he asked.

I didn't know what to say. If I told him the truth I might hurt his feelings, so I just shrugged my shoulders.

"Well, I wouldn't blame you if you were," he went on. "I'm sorry I've been as scarce as hen's teeth." That was another one of his funny expressions. "I just needed some time to sort out where I was going."

"And so now that you figured out that Northfield was where you wanted to go, is everything okay?" I asked.

"That's not what I meant by sorting out where I was going," he explained. "I meant I needed to figure out what I want to do with my life and what I want to be when I grow up."

It sure was confusing. First Mom, and now Dad. I'd thought my parents were already grown up.

"Well, I know what I want to be when I grow up,"

I said. "A teacher." The words just popped out—I didn't even know where they'd come from. I'd never thought about being a teacher before that minute, but it made sense. I liked teaching Trevor stuff, and I'd done a good job reading stories to that kid Jeremy.

"That's great, Joshua," Dad said.

"So, when you find out where you're going, will you take Mom and me along with you?" I asked.

"I don't know, Josh," he answered. "I can't make any promises right now. I need to earn some money to pay for my apartment. Speaking of which, we'd better get you there and into bed. You've had a long day."

"What are we having for Thanksgiving?" I asked.

"Well, if we had to depend on my cooking, it'd be peanut butter and jelly. So I'm taking you to a friend's house."

"What's his name?" I asked.

"Well, it's not a him," he answered.

"Whaddya mean?" I asked.

"Well, the friend is a lady. She's a secretary at the auto parts store."

My heart sank. I couldn't believe it. What would I tell Mom?

Then I remembered that I hadn't called her. She'd be worried. She knew what time the bus was supposed to get in.

"I've gotta call Mom," I said. "I promised I'd do it when I got here."

"There's a phone booth in the lobby," Dad said. "Here are some quarters."

I dropped the money in the slot and dialed our number. Mom must have been sitting right next to the phone. She picked it up in the middle of the first ring.

"Are you okay?" were her first words.

"I'm fine, Mom," I said. "The bus trip was good. I baby-sat for this little boy, and his mother bought me a hot fudge sundae."

"Have fun, honey," she said. "I'll see you at the bus station on Friday night. Bye."

Dad's apartment was tiny, but neat. His housekeeping habits had improved considerably since we lived in Woodview. The couch made into a bed. It was almost like magic. I brushed my teeth and hopped in.

What would tomorrow be like? Nobody could cook like my mom. I felt disloyal already, and I hadn't even met his friend.

The bus trip back home wasn't nearly as much fun as the first had been. Jeremy wasn't there to entertain me, and seeing my dad hadn't made me feel as good as I'd thought it would. Now, not only did I have to worry about Dad "figuring out where he was going," I had to think about his new friend Sally and how she fit in.

She was a nice-enough person. Not as pretty as Mom, of course, but okay. Sally had never cooked a turkey before, and it turned out dry and stringy, but she had a good sense of humor. The best part was the ice cream pie she had for dessert. She let me eat it in front of the TV—something Mom never lets me do.

The last hour of the trip dragged by. I counted telephone poles, blue cars, and license plates from other states. I tried to keep the three counts going separately, but after I'd counted eighty-seven telephone poles, I got confused and quit.

I didn't know what I was going to tell Mom about the trip. I'd just wait and see what she asked me. If I only answered her questions, I couldn't get into any trouble.

I spotted her car the minute the bus pulled into the lot. I was the first one out. With my balsa wood airplane clutched under my arm, I ran to her.

"Well, you look like you're glad to be home," she said.

"I am," I agreed.

"Did you have a good time?"

"Yeah."

"Did your father cook Thanksgiving dinner?" she asked.

She was getting close to a dangerous subject. I remembered my idea of only answering the questions I was asked.

"No," I said.

"So, what did you have to eat?" she probed.

"Turkey," I said.

"Did you go to a restaurant?"

"No," I answered.

"Joshua McIntire," she said sternly. "Are we playing that old question-and-answer game again? Where did you eat Thanksgiving dinner?"

"At a friend of dad's," I said.

"Was this a lady friend?" she asked.

"Yeah," I said.

"Oh, Joshua," she said softly, "that must have been hard for you."

I didn't know what to say. I felt like crying, but I didn't want to make her feel bad too.

"Was she nice?" she asked.

"Not as nice as you," I answered. I had tears in my eyes.

"Joshua, you are not to worry about this," she said. "Your father and I are divorced, and he is living his own life."

"But if he has a girlfriend, that means he's not coming back," I said.

"You're probably right, Joshua, but it's time you accepted that. It's not your fault that it happened, and you can't do anything to patch it up again."

"But I've been praying," I said. "And I just know God will answer my prayers."

"Oh, Joshua," Mom said with a big sigh. "I think you should pray for help in accepting what's happened.

We've got lots of good things to look forward to."

"Like what?" I asked.

"Like dinner out tonight, for one," she said.

"Where are we going?" I asked.

"Well, actually, you and I are being taken out to dinner," she said.

"By who?" I asked.

"By whom," she corrected me. "Sonny Studebaker called me at the office this afternoon and asked if I thought you'd like to be welcomed home in style. I said I thought you'd like that a lot."

My life was happening so fast I couldn't keep up with it.

"There's another piece of news I think you'll be interested in, too," she went on. "It involves your friend Ben Anderson."

"What did he do?" I asked.

"He was caught breaking into the Klum house after they boarded it up. It seems the police caught him with some artifacts he'd dug up in a cave there."

"I know all about that, Mom. He showed the stuff to me and wanted me to go back with him. Boy, am I glad I said no."

Mom smiled. "There are times, Joshua, when you *are* very, very good. Just like the girl with the curl in the middle of her forehead." She squeezed my arm.

"Aw, Mom," I said, "don't get mushy on me."

91

"That is my privilege as a mother, Joshua," she said firmly. "But what are we doing standing around this bus station? We've got to get home and get dressed. I haven't been out to dinner with two handsome men for quite a while."

It took a minute for what she'd said to register. Had I heard her correctly? She thought Sonny was handsome? Oh, boy! I breathed a quick prayer. *Dear God*, I thought, *do You know any good books about raising parents?*

Be sure to read about Josh in his next adventure, *Operation Garbage.*

While I was washing my hands, the door opened. The man who came in looked like a commuter. I was drying my hands.

"You're a good-looking young man. Can I buy you something to eat?"

My heart stopped. I didn't need a neon sign to tell me that this was "Mr. Stranger Danger." But he looked so nice. He was wearing shoes with little tassels on them and tortoise shell glasses like my dad's.

The man stood between me and the door. He smiled and spoke again. "You're alone, aren't you?"

My feet felt like they were glued to the ceramic tiles of the men's room. I could hear my heart pounding like jungle drums. I needed to do something fast. I had to get out of there. I walked toward the door, and he didn't move. Then somehow I found my running legs and darted around him. I pushed the door outward and burst into the station, heading I didn't know where.